KU-428-625

Beast Quest®

www.beastquest.co.uk

ORCHARD BOOKS

Early reader editions of *Vedra & Krimon, Kragos & Kildor, Arax, Creta, Mortaxe* and *Ravira* first published in Great Britain in 2014, 2015, 2016 by Orchard Books
This collection published in 2016 by The Watts Publishing Group

1 3 5 7 9 10 8 6 4 2

A CIP catalogue record for this book is available from the British Library.

ISBN 978 1 40834 547 4

Printed in China

The paper and board used in this book are made from wood from responsible sources

Orchard Books
An imprint of Hachette Children's Group
Part of The Watts Publishing Group Limited
Carmelite House, 50 Victoria Embankment, London EC4Y 0DZ

An Hachette UK Company
www.hachette.co.uk
www.hachettechildrens.co.uk

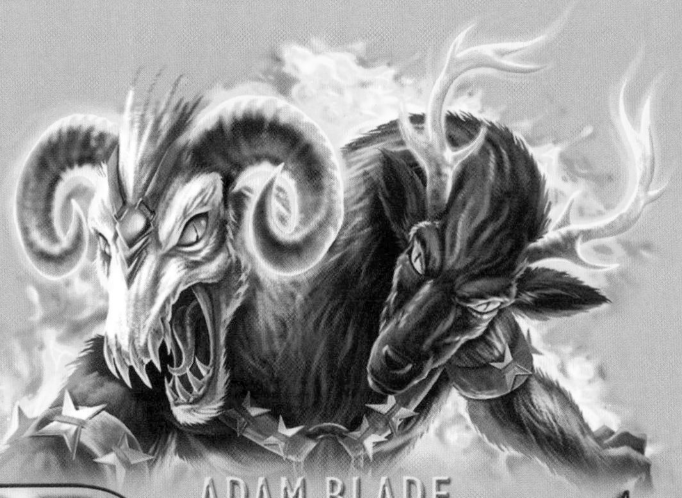

ADAM BLADE

Beast Quest®

THE ULTIMATE STORY COLLECTION

CONTENTS

TOM

Heroic fighter of Beasts and saviour of Avantia

ELENNA

Tom's trusted friend and loyal companion

STORM

Tom's brave stallion

SILVER

Elenna's pet wolf

KING HUGO
King of Avantia
ADURO
The Good Wizard who serves King Hugo and guides Tom
MALVEL
The Dark Wizard. He is Tom's main enemy

THE ICY PLAINS
THE NORTHERN MOUNTAINS
THE CENTRAL PLAINS
WESTERN OCEAN
THE FOREST OF FEAR
GRASSY PLAINS
THE WINDING RIVER
THE RUBY DESERT
SPINDREL

MAP OF AVANTIA

THE PIT OF FIRE

MALVEL'S MAZE

STONEWIN VOLCANO

THE DEAD VALLEY

ERRINEL

THE DEAD JUNGLE

THE DARK WOOD

THE DARK JUNGLE

THE PIT
MALVEL'S
THE NIDREM CAVES
THE RIVER DOUR
KING HUGO'S PALACE
THE CITY

MAP OF RION

AVANTIA

Vedra and Krimon

Twin Beasts of Avantia

WELCOME TO THE KINGDOM OF AVANTIA, where magical Beasts protect the land. I am Aduro, a Good Wizard. Twin dragons, Vedra and Krimon, have been born and are in danger from the Evil Wizard, Malvel. Our brave young heroes, Tom and Elenna, have helped before. Can they keep these Beasts safe from harm? Read on to find out!

PART ONE

TWIN BEASTS

TWIN BEASTS

At the Royal Palace of Avantia a birthday party for King Hugo was taking place. As Tom and his friend Elenna raised their glasses in a toast, Elenna whispered in Tom's ear, "Here's to the six beasts of Avantia!"

"Shhh!" warned Tom. Most people believed the Beasts that protected the land were only a legend. But Tom and Elenna had seen them, and freed them from Malvel, the Dark Wizard.

The Good Wizard, Aduro, led the friends away from the party and spoke solemnly to them.

Twin Beasts

"Two new Beasts have been created," said Aduro. "They are twin dragons, and their names are Vedra and Krimon."

"Baby dragons!" gasped Elenna, excited. But Aduro was not smiling.

"Their birth could put Avantia in danger," he said, and conjured an image on the wall. It showed the two dragons sleeping in a dark cave. One was green and the other red. Tom and Elenna gazed at the dragons, enchanted.

"Vedra is green and Krimon is red,"

began Aduro as the vision faded. "It is rare for two Beasts to be created together. If Malvel hears about the twins, he will use them for evil purposes and harm Avantia. Will you help to protect the dragons and stop Malvel?"

"Of course we will!" promised Tom and Elenna.

The wizard led Tom and Elenna to a room with a huge wooden chest in the middle. Next to it lay Tom's shield and sword, along with Elenna's bow and a quiver of arrows.

Aduro climbed inside. Puzzled, Tom followed, with his sword and shield. His shield was decorated with powerful tokens from their previous Quests which would protect them. Elenna followed with her bow and arrows.

The bottom of the chest slid away to reveal a stairway down to a rushing river. A small rowing boat waited there.

"This is the hidden River Dour," Aduro said to Tom. "The river will take you to the dragons' cave. You and Elenna must go alone."

"What shall we do when we get there?" asked Tom.

"Find Vedra and Krimon," Aduro instructed,

"and take them north, to Rion, where they will be safe. You must arrive before the full moon, or Malvel will cast his wicked spell on the dragons."

Aduro held up Tom's sword and whispered an enchantment. "If Malvel finds the dragons before you do, touch the Beasts' underbellies with your sword to rescue them," he said.

Tom and Elenna climbed bravely into the boat, taking a bundle Aduro produced from beneath his robes.

"Food, drink and warm cloaks," he said, and waved them off down the dark river into the unknown.

For hours, the water churned all around them.

"Rocks!" Tom gasped suddenly, as they fought

to steer the boat safely. Tom knew that the splinter of Sepron's tooth in his shield would protect them from water, but not rocks!

Far ahead, they saw a faint light, like a steady flame. It grew stronger as the water became calm and the little boat floated gently into a wide underground lake.

Twin Beasts

"Look!" gasped Tom, pointing. A large creature was swimming towards them.

"It's Sepron!" Elenna shouted joyfully. The huge sea serpent let out a cry of welcome.

Slowly, they became aware of the other Beasts. Stepping ashore, they saw Arcta the Mountain Giant peering down at them.

The huge fire dragon, Ferno, stood nearby as Nanook the Snow Monster and Epos the Flame Bird welcomed them. Clopping hooves announced the arrival of Tagus the Horse-Man.

He picked up Tom and Elenna and cantered away, followed by the other friendly Beasts.

After a short ride, Tagus stopped and they got down. There were two newborn dragons lying in a nest of golden straw.

"We have to protect these trusting Beasts," Tom whispered, as Vedra began gently pecking at Elenna's hair.

Tom pulled the magical map from beneath his shirt. Aduro had given it to him when he began his very first Quest. Unfolding the parchment, he saw snow-covered mountains rise up in sharp points. The map was alive! A tiny light showed where they had found the dragons. A slender golden path led northwards. It was pointing the way to the snowy land of Rion.

Elenna rushed to get the food and the cloaks, while Tom spoke to the baby dragons.

"I'm here to protect you," he began.

"*We* are here to protect them, you mean," said Elenna, returning with their things.

With a heavy flapping of wings, Ferno and Epos rose into the air, circling the cave. Ferno carried Elenna and Vedra, while Tom and Krimon clung to Epos's back. Aduro's cloaks kept them warm as the great creatures flew north above the wintry landscape.

It was early afternoon when Tom saw high mountains ahead. He looked at the map, and a golden glow showed that they were close to Rion.

Then Tom noticed that one mountain was different from the others. It had a crater that glowed with a fierce red fire.

"It's a volcano!" Tom shouted.

Epos let out a croak of alarm as molten rock gushed up into the air. Tom saw Elenna and Vedra struggle to hold onto Ferno's back as he swerved to avoid the fountain of fire. He threw his shield up and the magical dragon scale on it saved them from the fiery rock, but as Ferno turned, Elenna's bow and arrows fell into the flaming crater.

Epos tried hard to pull back, and Tom felt himself slipping.

"No!" he cried, falling from Epos's back.

He plunged helplessly downwards. A rushing sound filled his ears until, suddenly, Epos caught him with a triumphant shriek.

Exhausted and dazed, they flew on until the volcano was far behind them. At last Epos and

Ferno landed on a remote slab of rock where, strangely, a boy was curled up as if asleep. As they approached, his eyes snapped open and he jumped to his feet.

"My name is Seth," he said, smiling and holding out his hand. But as Tom reached out his own hand, the boy lunged forwards, and threw him to the ground. Gasping for breath, Tom saw that Seth had a bronze sword in his hand, and it was pointed at his throat.

Tom twisted to one side as the sword struck the rock close to his head. Seth stumbled forwards and Tom jumped up. Sparks flew as their swords clashed again and again, the noise echoing around the mountain peaks that surrounded them.

At last, Tom was able to kick the blade out of Seth's grip, and point his own sword at the boy's neck.

"I'm sorry!" Seth gasped. "I didn't mean to hurt you. I was half crazy with hunger and fear."

Tom picked up the bronze sword and slipped it neatly into his own belt before allowing Seth to stand up.

Elenna gave Seth some bread to eat. The boy explained how he had become separated from the rest of his party while out hunting.

Tom and Elenna exchanged a wary look but Seth seemed so tired and frail they decided to give him another chance.

Seth spotted Epos and Ferno. "These must be two of the legendary Beasts of Avantia!" he said, gasping again.

"No one is meant to know," Elenna said, panicking. "The Beasts should never be seen."

"I live in Rion," Seth said. "If you take me home, I promise I will never speak of these Beasts to anyone!"

Tom climbed up onto Epos's back and helped Seth up in front of him. Krimon belched a little fire at him, to make sure the boy kept his distance.

Soon they were flying high again, and Tom saw the landscape begin to change. Blue lakes glowed in the valleys and gushing rivers roared by.

"We're in Rion!" Tom called back to Elenna when he had checked his map.

Spying a clearing, Elenna and Ferno swooped down, but as Epos prepared to follow, Tom saw Seth take a small leather pouch of golden powder from his jacket.

"The deadly magic of Malvel!" roared Seth, his eyes burning bright.

"No!" Tom shouted, as Seth leaned forward and hurled golden dust into Epos's eyes. The bird let out a deafening croak as Seth laughed.

He threw more of the dust into Tom's face. The golden powder filled Tom's eyes, stinging badly.

He was blinded as Epos fell to the ground and crash-landed.

Tom stumbled helplessly across the snowy ground, calling out for Elenna.

"Stay there," she said, when she had rushed over to him. "I'll get some water from the river for your eyes."

Tom listened to the noises of the frightened Beasts. A moment later, he felt icy water splash onto his face and cautiously opened his eyes.

There was a golden glow at the edges of Tom's vision but at least he could see again.

Seth and his bronze sword had both disappeared.

Back at the clearing, Epos was shaking her head from side to side, trying to clear the dust from her eyes. Krimon came creeping from where he had been hiding under Ferno's wing.

"Where has Vedra gone?" Elenna gasped, her eyes searching around desperately.

"Seth must have taken him," Tom replied, his voice full of anger and guilt.

A deep hollow laugh echoed across the treetops. It was the Dark Wizard, Malvel.

HELLO AGAIN, MY FRIENDS. TOM AND Elenna's Quest is far from over! Malvel is close by and his servant, Seth, has stolen Vedra away. Both young dragons are in danger. There is much to do before the full moon rises tonight.

PART TWO

DANGER IN RION

DANGER IN RION

TOM STARED GRIMLY INTO THE HOWLING blizzard. Epos was recovering from Seth's evil attack, but it would be a while before she could fly again. Ferno crawled closer to Epos, lifting one wing to protect her. Krimon had been huddled up against Ferno's side, but now he suddenly stood up and headed towards the forest.

"I think he can sense his brother," Tom said. "Let's go after him."

Tom and Elenna followed Krimon. He snorted and carried on, trotting deeper into the dark forest.

Danger in Rion

Krimon paused and closed his eyes. A long bright flame streamed upwards from his nostrils and hung in the air, gradually changing into a bright fireball. At the same time, an orange glow was spreading over his leathery skin.

Over his heart there shone a patch of emerald-green light as strong as the fireball.

"What does it mean?" whispered Elenna.

"I think it shows the bond between the two baby dragons," Tom replied. "They're linked in some way."

Danger in Rion

Tom and Elenna followed Krimon as, with a snort, the dragon ran back into the wood. The glowing fireball moved along in front of them as the Beast's heart throbbed with light.

The dragon stopped suddenly in front of a great hedge of holly that blocked their way. Its branches were as thick as Tom's arms. Krimon was confused and ran up and down as the mocking laughter of Malvel echoed around the snowy forest. Krimon's brother was on the other side of that massive hedge, but there was no way through. Tom drew his sword and began to hack at the spiky bushes.

Tom's muscles ached with the effort of battling his way through the vicious holly.

He could see no end to the tangle of branches. After a while, exhaustion overcame him.

"We have to get through somehow," said Tom desperately. "If Malvel puts his spell on the dragons when the moon is full, they will be Evil for ever – and we won't be able to save them."

Suddenly, as if he understood, Krimon pushed his head into the hole Tom had made in the hedge. A burst of orange flame came pouring from the Beast's mouth.

"He's burning his way through!" Elenna cried.

Tom and Elenna followed Krimon through the gap he had burnt in the hedge to the other side. Before them there were paths leading through rows of more holly bushes.

Danger in Rion

But which of the paths should they take?

The orange glow on Krimon's chest had become pale and the ball of flame in front of them was even dimmer. Tom knew this must mean Vedra was far away.

Krimon ran on, trying different paths until the light on his chest and the ball of fire brightened.

They were getting closer to Vedra!

Suddenly, Elenna gave a yelp of alarm as a flash of fire appeared in front of her. As they watched, more flashes appeared along the path.

"I don't like this," Elenna said. "These lights aren't here to help us. This is Dark Magic."

"Get back!" Tom shouted suddenly, leaping in front of Elenna as a monstrous human-shaped creature reared above them.

Tom raised his sword at the monster. It was dark green, with long claws, sharp teeth and eyes that glowed red like boiling blood.

Then Tom realised the creature wasn't moving.

"It's just a statue!" Tom said, turning to Elenna with a grin.

The hedges were filled with many similar hideous statues, all half-hidden by holly.

The brave friends plunged onwards, until they came to two pathways exactly alike.

Krimon chose the right-hand path. Tom and Elenna followed, but straight away they were surrounded by a swirling green mist.

Tom began to feel a terrible pain in his head and closed his eyes. When he opened them again, Malvel was standing there.

Tom ran at the Dark Wizard, his sword raised.

"I have to fight him!" he shouted to Elenna.

"There's no one there!" she said with a gasp. "It's the pain in your head and the green mist.

They're making you see things."

Slowly, Tom calmed down. "Malvel must be using that green mist to control me," he said quietly. "I can't trust my own eyes."

Tom and Elenna ran on after Krimon, finding him in front of a great door that blocked the path. The door had no handle. Tom thrust at it with his shield and kicked it with all his strength until, at last, it swung open. On the other side there was just another snowy path.

"I hate this place!" screamed Tom suddenly, swinging his sword towards Elenna. Then he suddenly realised what he was doing.

"I'm sorry!" he cried, falling to his knees.

"Something is making you behave like this."

Elenna's voice was calm. "You have to fight it, Tom, or Malvel will win."

Tom, Elenna and Krimon trudged through the snow until they reached a wide chasm. While Tom and Elenna wondered how they would ever get across, Krimon spread his wings and took a giant leap, then landed safely on the far side.

Thinking fast, Tom cut a branch from the hedge and sliced off the smaller twigs until he had made a smooth pole twice his height.

As Elenna watched in amazement, Tom took a deep breath and then ran forward. The pole hit the ground and Tom sprang into the air and over the gap, landing safely beside Krimon.

He threw the pole back to Elenna and soon she was standing beside him.

Continuing along the snowy path, Tom noticed that Krimon had begun to whine as if in pain. Finally, he fell to the ground.

"What's happening?" Elenna asked, trying to comfort the Beast.

Tom sank to his knees beside the young dragon, feeling panic rising in his chest.

"Something bad must be happening to Vedra. Krimon is suffering the same pain!"

Suddenly the fireball over Krimon's head went out, and the orange and green glow on his chest disappeared.

"The link between Vedra and Krimon has been broken," Tom said sadly. "Something awful must have happened."

Without the dragon to guide them, how would they get to the heart of the maze?

"What are we going to do now?" Elenna asked, tears shining in her eyes.

Tom racked his brains for an answer, but Malvel's Dark Magic was playing tricks on him again. Then Tom heard a dragon whimpering.

"Be quiet!" Tom shouted at Krimon.

"Tom!" Elenna frowned. "He isn't making a sound."

Tom looked at Krimon. Elenna was right.

"It's Vedra!" he said, suddenly realising where the sound was coming from.

"What do you mean? I can't hear anything," Elenna said, confused.

"He's this way!" Tom said, running down the path. Elenna and Krimon followed behind.

With Tom in the lead, they turned a final bend and stumbled into a wide circular clearing. Vedra was there in the centre, held by a thick spiked chain. Seth stood a little distance away, smiling evilly.

Danger in Rion

Krimon ran to greet Vedra and Seth magically removed the green dragon's chains. Vedra reared up and spat fire towards his brother. Malvel's Dark Magic was in the Beast's blood. Tom was too late.

"Vedra is ours!" Seth cried, sending Tom's sword to the ground with his own blade.

Tom hurled his shield at Seth, knocking him down.

Danger in Rion

Elenna ran to stop Seth getting away. Then she stooped to snatch the bronze sword from Seth's fingers.

"Go and help Krimon!" she called, throwing Tom the sword.

Watching the dragons fight was terrifying. The moon was high in the sky and time was running out. Tom remembered Aduro's words. He had to touch Vedra's underbelly with the tip of his sword. He ran in close but his sword struck Vedra's foreleg. The metal rang uselessly against the dragon's hard scales.

Tom stared at the silver moon and a plan formed in his mind. He tilted his sword so that its blade caught the moon's reflection.

A flash of light struck Vedra in the eyes. Dazzled, the Beast reared up and Tom sprang forward to touch his belly with the sword.

Tom stood firm, blinded by a sudden wind.

Then he opened his eyes.

Vedra and Krimon were beside him. Elenna was nearby, but Seth and the bronze sword were gone.

"We did it!" Tom said, with a grin. The dragons were recovering. Vedra was safe from harm, cured of Malvel's evil.

Tom brought the magic map out of his tunic and unrolled it. "We're in the middle of nowhere!" he groaned.

"Look!" said Elenna, pointing into the sky. Their friends Ferno and Epos were winging their way towards them over the snowy forest.

When Ferno and Epos landed, the twins clambered onto Ferno's back and the great dragon took off into the skies again. They flew away towards Rion.

Tom and Elenna climbed onto Epos's back. Tom looked again at the map, and a shimmering

face appeared. It was Aduro the wizard.

"Thanks to you, the twin dragons will grow up in a place of safety," he said, smiling. "Ferno will stay by their side to teach and protect them."

Epos launched herself into the night sky, and sped southwards. Tom had succeeded in his quest and the twin Beasts of Avantia were safe. Now they could go home.

Home to Avantia.

Kragos and Kildor
The Two-headed Demon

MY NAME IS TALADON. WELCOME TO THE kingdom of Avantia, which is now a place of peace, free of Dark Magic. The people are celebrating but in my heart I sense that the Dark Wizard, Malvel is plotting to tear Avantia apart. Can my brave son, Tom, stop him and save the kingdom?

PART ONE

A FIERY SECRET

A FIERY SECRET

TOM THUNDERED ALONG ON HIS BLACK stallion, Storm, with his friend Elenna behind him. His father, Taladon, rode beside him across the green hills of Avantia.

They reached a house, got down from the horses and knocked on the door. Tom's Aunt Maria answered it.

"Taladon!" Aunt Maria cried, drawing him into a hug. "Where have you been?"

"It's a long story," began Taladon. "I was kidnapped by the Dark Wizard, Malvel.

I escaped when Tom wounded Malvel. He saved the Amulet of Avantia and banished Malvel from the country. Tom is a hero!"

"Tom! Elenna! You're safe!" Aunt Maria continued, as tears welled up in her eyes. "I'm so proud of you both."

Elenna settled the horses and her grey wolf, Silver, as Tom led the way out to the forge.

"Uncle Henry," he said, as he opened the door. "There's someone to see you."

Henry's mouth gaped wide. "Taladon!" he gasped. "It's wonderful to have you home."

That night, a loud crash woke Tom. He dragged on his tunic and dashed outside to see a huge hole in the forge door.

When Tom looked around, he saw a golden flicker in the trees.

"What's that?" he whispered to Elenna and Taladon, once they had caught up with him.

A Fiery Secret

Tom's heart started to thump as a creature came into view. It had one body, but two heads. One of them was like a ram, while the other was like a stag. Golden flames licked all around, so that it stood inside a shimmering light.

The Beast gave a roar and raced away into the forest.

"Keep back, and guard the cottage!" Taladon said. He ran into the trees after the creature.

"Do you think the Beast is one of Malvel's servants, sent to hurt us?" Tom said.

Before Elenna could reply, Tom's father reappeared. He strode quickly towards the forge. There was panic and anger in his eyes.

They quickly followed and saw him plunge one hand into the flames of the forge. The fire was fierce and he screwed up his face in pain but he did not hesitate. He seemed to be searching for something.

Uncle Henry managed to drag his brother away.

A Fiery Secret

"What's going on?" Tom rushed to his father's side. "Why did you do that?"

"The Cup of Life has been stolen!" was all Taladon could say.

"What is the Cup of Life?" Elenna asked.

"It is a magic goblet," said Taladon.

"Anyone who drinks from it can repel death," he continued, through teeth clenched in pain. "Years ago, King Hugo gave me the cup to guard. Because it has to be kept in fire, I placed it right here, in the forge."

Elenna nodded. "If Malvel drinks from it he'll be strong again. And he could launch another attack on Avantia."

"The cup must be rescued. We must leave right away," Tom said to Elenna.

Taladon knew he would not be able to help his son because of his burnt hand. Aunt Maria would look after him.

Tom and Elenna mounted Storm and set off with Silver. On the outskirts of the forest, they heard a rustle, then relaxed when they saw a young deer step towards them.

"No, Silver." Elenna frowned as the wolf growled. "He's not dangerous."

Elenna walked beside Silver as they went deeper into the forest. The little deer followed a few paces behind.

"Look there!" Elenna exclaimed at last. She pointed at some huge cloven hoof marks beside the path.

As the footprints led them deeper into the forest, Tom noticed that the trees ahead were lit up by a strange, pale silvery light.

Outlined in shimmering silver was the image of a man.

"Aduro!" Tom exclaimed. He rushed towards the vision, as he recognised the man.

It was the Good Wizard, Aduro. "My strength is fading," he told them in a weak, shaky voice.

A Fiery Secret

"Avantia is in great danger. You must find the Cup of Life."

A terrible feeling of horror hit Tom.

Aduro continued. "If the Cup of Life is not found by the next full moon, Avantia's leaders will lose their powers for ever.

King Hugo and I will be stranded between life and death."

"But then Malvel could take over Avantia!" Tom cried.

"The full moon is only three nights away!" Elenna added.

"The Beast's name is Kragos and Kildor."

Aduro spoke slowly. "It has two names because it is a Beast of two natures." He waved his arms weakly. A picture of a two-headed Beast appeared in the air between them. One part was a wolf, the other a fox with cunning eyes. The image flickered and a new one appeared. This time it looked like the Beast Tom and Elenna had seen, with one stag's head and one ram's head.

"Kragos and Kildor change their form with every generation," Aduro told them. "But whatever the form, they will always attack."

The vision of Aduro faded. Tom, Elenna and the animals followed the Beast's tracks. The little deer still trotted along beside them.

Gradually, Tom noticed that the forest around them was changing. The ground was softer, and the air was warmer. The trees grew even closer together and thick vines hung from the branches.

"It isn't safe to carry on. We need to make camp," Elenna said, as it grew dark.

They got down from Storm's back and Tom noticed that the little deer had disappeared.

"What's happened to our new friend?" he asked.

Tom and Elenna began to look around for the deer. Then a squeal of fear came from the darkness.

"That's him!" said Tom, and he rushed towards the sound. He chopped his way through the thick bushes until he could see the frightened animal.

At last Tom reached the place where the deer was trapped. There were vines tangled around its legs. The deer was watching Tom and Elenna with a strange glint in its eye.

Tom swung his sword back and struck at the vine in front of him, but the ends whipped back at him.

"The vines are alive!" Tom cried, as they lunged towards him. Now he was caught in the vines. The little deer's eyes glowed with triumph.

He led me here deliberately! Tom thought, as he struggled to free himself. *But why?*

The vines dragged Tom into the undergrowth and his sword fell from his hand. When he twisted round, he saw Elenna grab it and chase after him.

"Don't give up!" she called.

Suddenly Tom saw a huge green pod. He yelled as the vines swung him up through the air and dropped him into a pool of poisonous liquid inside.

"Elenna! Help!" he cried, as sharp teeth slid from the walls and fastened onto his body. The plant was eating Tom alive!

Suddenly, a sword blade stabbed through the pod and tore a hole big enough for him to clamber through.

But Tom and Elenna were still not safe. Just then the deer leapt into the open. Tom spun round and saw it grow larger. Antlers sprouted from its head as it turned into a mighty stag.

"It's Kragos!" Elenna said.

"The little deer must have been Kragos in disguise!" said Tom. He remembered Aduro explaining that this Beast had two parts.

"Kragos and Kildor have split themselves," Tom said. "The tracks we followed must belong to Kildor, the ram part."

"And he still has the Cup of Life," said Elenna.

A Fiery Secret

"We must stop him!"

"Take Storm and Silver somewhere safe," Tom whispered to Elenna.

Kragos charged at Tom. He staggered, but managed to jab his sword into the stag's side.

Kragos bellowed in pain, but then came another sound. It was the sound of a group of hunters on horseback. Their horses crashed through the undergrowth. The hunters fired a flurry of arrows, which zipped through the air. Tom lay flat as the hunters raced after Kragos – who they thought was just an ordinary stag.

"No!" cried Tom in frustration, as Kragos charged away. "I almost had him!"

Tom picked himself up and Elenna emerged from the trees. He noticed there was blood trickling down her arm.

"One of the hunters' arrows grazed me," she told him.

From his shield, Tom carefully took a talon that had been given to him by the magical firebird, Epos. It had incredible healing powers. He held the talon to Elenna's arm, but nothing happened.

"It isn't working," Tom said sadly. He bandaged her arm instead.

"I'll be fine," Elenna assured him as they set off again. The hunters' horses had churned up the earth and destroyed Kildor's tracks.

"We'll never be able to find him now," said Tom with a sigh. "How will we know where to find the Cup of Life?"

As Tom spoke, a dim light appeared among the trees.

Tom could just make out the figures of Wizard Aduro and King Hugo. They both looked exhausted, their eyes dead.

"I think," whispered Tom, "that Wizard Aduro is sending us a vision of what will happen if we fail in our Quest."

Elenna shuddered.

"He's telling us that we mustn't give up," Tom went on.

As the vision faded, Tom had an idea. He fished in his pocket and brought out his father's magical compass.

"Look!" Tom said to Elenna, pointing. "The compass says we must go to the Ruby Desert!"

MALVEL IS SEARCHING FOR A WAY BACK into Avantia. He has sent his two-headed Beast, Kragos and Kildor, to do his bidding. Now that they have the Cup of Life, Avantia is in terrible danger.

PART TWO

DESTINY IN THE DESERT

DESTINY IN THE DESERT

Tom and Elenna were riding towards the desert to search for the Cup of Life. It was very hot.

"We must find water," Tom said to Elenna, who sat behind him. They were both feeling weak now.

Tom turned Storm towards a town he remembered from a previous deadly Quest. He knew there was a well there so they could all rest and drink. The road plunged into a deep ravine with rock rising high up on either side.

Tom patted his faithful horse's neck. "Just one good gallop, Storm," he said. "When we get there, you can have all the water you want."

Storm raced along the rocky track. Sparks flew up from his shoed hooves. Elenna clung tightly to Tom's waist, and Silver bounded alongside.

"Go, boy!" Tom shouted.

The end of the ravine, where the path plunged back into bright sunlight, was getting closer.

Suddenly, Tom heard a rumble like distant thunder. A huge section of the cliff face had torn free. Great rocks were sliding downwards, carrying earth and trees with them.

"No!" Tom yelled. He knew there was no time

to outrun the landslide. He pulled on Storm's reins with all his strength and managed to turn the horse back the way they had come.

There was a booming sound, and an avalanche of rocks crashed down. Silver was knocked off his feet but somehow managed to scramble free again.

The four friends were safe, but the road they had meant to take was now completely blocked by rocks. Tom wondered how they would get through. Then he remembered the purple jewel he had won when he defeated Sting the Scorpion Man. The jewel had the magical power to cut through rock.

Tom pulled the gleaming jewel from his belt.

He held it to the rocks. Purple light glowed from the gem and there was a loud creak.

Tom stared in wonder as a huge boulder began to crumble.

"It's working!" Elenna said, grinning widely.

With the power of the jewel they cleared a path through the boulders. Soon they were on their way again.

When they reached the town, they rested by the well and drank thirstily. A man leading a horse and a mule came to drink too. Tom had an important question for him.

"What's the hottest place in the desert?" he asked, remembering what his father had said. The Cup of Life had to be placed in fire before

its magic would work again.

"The Valley of Eternal Flame," the man replied. "The fire there never goes out."

Excitement surged through Tom. Now they would soon get back the Cup of Life!

The sun was beating down on Tom, Elenna,

Storm and Silver as they headed into the desert. Before long, the heat began to drain Elenna's strength and her eyes started to flicker.

"My arm feels worse," she said at last, sounding faint.

Tom was worried. He got down from Storm and helped Elenna down beside him. When he removed the bandage, he saw that the cut had stopped bleeding, but it had turned a deep grey colour. All around it, Elenna's arm was turning red.

"The arrow must have been poisoned," Tom said quietly. He was shocked and afraid for his friend.

"I'm strong," Elenna assured him. "I can fight

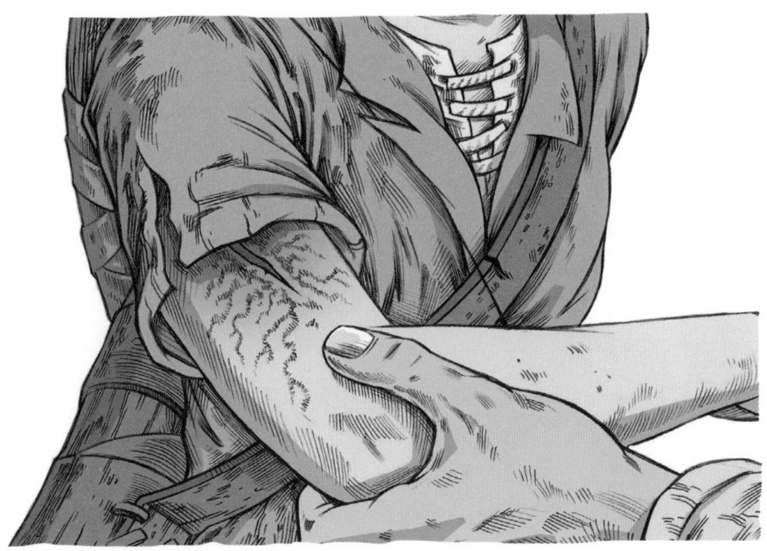

it off until we return to Errinel. Aunt Maria will know what to do."

Tom was not so sure.

Suddenly, Silver gave an excited yelp. Tom saw the wolf digging at the roots of a bush with green leaves.

"He's found something," Elenna said.

"That's sagebrush!" Tom exclaimed. "Aunt Maria uses the root to treat scrapes and scratches. Well done, Silver!"

Tom dashed over to the bush and helped the grey wolf to dig until enough sand was cleared away from the roots. Tom took out his knife and cut away a piece of the root. He used his knife to cut it open and squeezed the juices onto Elenna's wound.

Her arm didn't look any different but Elenna sighed. "That feels so much better!" she said, and gave Silver a big hug.

Tom cut some more of the sagebrush root and tucked it into his saddlebag, just in case.

"Let's go!" Tom said. "It can't be far now!"

The air grew even hotter as Tom and Elenna ventured further into the desert. At last Tom spotted a dot of light on the horizon. As they drew closer, he could see it was a patch of burning cacti.

"The heat's so great that it even sets the cacti on fire," Tom said, shocked. "That means we must be on the right track."

When the sun went down, the temperature dropped and an icy wind began to blow. Elenna wanted to rest, but Tom was frightened. She was still not well. *If she goes to sleep in these freezing conditions,* he thought, *she might never wake up.*

The friends carried on. They were all tired, but Tom knew he must stay alert. Kragos and Kildor might be lurking nearby.

The moon set, leaving them to make their way by starlight. When the sun came up, waves of fierce heat rolled out to meet them. *We must be close now.*

They pushed their way through a path of huge boulders. Tom gasped when he saw what lay beyond. It was a huge pit, with flames roaring up from it. Nestling in the heart of the fire was the Cup of Life.

Tom had taken only one step towards the pit when he heard a great roar. It was a huge ram. It charged at him from behind another massive boulder.

"Kildor!" Tom exclaimed.

Brave Elenna fired an arrow at the creature, as the Beast reared up on his hind legs and battered Tom's shield. He lunged forwards and drove his sword into the ram's side. There was a bellowing sound and Tom saw Kragos gallop into sight. The two animals charged wildly at each other, and their horns and antlers clashed together.

Then the creatures' bodies melted magically into each other to form one terrifying Beast.

Destiny in the Desert

The Beast wore a thick leather belt studded with razor-sharp silver discs. It removed one of the discs and hurled it straight at Tom. Suddenly, there were more and more of the weapons spinning through the air. Leaping nimbly from

side to side, Tom managed to dodge most of the sharp objects. Then one struck his shoulder. He felt a sharp pain and saw blood running down his arm.

Tom heard Elenna calling out. "Over here, Beast!" she said, her voice hoarse with pain.

Kragos and Kildor bellowed fiercely as they prepared to attack Elenna before she could fire her arrow.

Tom swiftly ran to meet Kragos and Kildor as they charged towards Elenna, then slipped aside and began to run around them as fast as he could. The double Beast let out a roar of anger and frustration. It turned in circles, trying to attack Tom. Soon he could see that both heads

were getting dizzy. Bravely using one of Kildor's knees to help him, Tom sprang up and tumbled high over their heads. Both Beasts tried to attack him, tangling their horns and antlers horribly in the struggle. They were locked together, staggering as they tried to separate themselves.

The Beast bellowed with fury and shook its heads. Tom saw Elenna kneeling at the edge of the pit of fire. She carefully poured the last of their water onto her handkerchief and wrapped it around her hand to protect herself. Then she reached into the fire and lifted out the Cup of Life.

Before Tom could say anything, a roar of rage echoed from the sky.

"It's Malvel!" Tom cried.

The roar of the defeated wizard went on and on. Kragos and Kildor stopped struggling. Then Tom saw their body began to disintegrate. Soon the twin Beasts were no more than a heap of sand.

Elenna held out the Cup of Life and Tom ran towards her.

"I've got the cup!" she exclaimed, before collapsing on the ground.

Horror surged through Tom as he looked into Elenna's face. *She's dying!* he thought.

He unwrapped the damp handkerchief from Elenna's hand. He reached for the now-cooled Cup of Life, and managed to squeeze a few drops of water into it.

"Come on, Elenna," he said gently. "You must drink this, and then we have to get home. Our Quest is over."

He tilted the cup against her lips and let the few drops of water trickle into her mouth.

Slowly, Elenna opened her eyes and looked at her wounded arm. There was not even a scar!

"The Cup of Life really works!" she said, laughing with surprise.

"It really does," Tom agreed, and gave a grin. Just then, a blue light shimmered in front of them, and the Wizard Aduro appeared.

There was fire flashing from his fingers. Tom took a step back as the Cup of Life vanished.

"It has returned to your uncle's forge," Aduro explained. "And now you must return too."

The light flashed again. When it faded, Aduro had gone, and the desert had been replaced by the green grass of Errinel.

Destiny in the Desert

Tom and Elenna led the animals towards the village.

When they reached the village square, Tom and Elenna stopped, staring in surprise.

A long table heaped with food stretched in front of them. Many of the villagers were seated at the table.

"Welcome home!" cried Aunt Maria. She ran over and hugged them close. Taladon and Uncle Henry rushed over too, and all the villagers started cheering.

Tom was filled with pride to think that he and Elenna had saved this happy village and the rest of Avantia from the plots of the Dark Wizard, Malvel.

Creta
The Winged Terror

I AM MARC, APPRENTICE TO THE GOOD Wizard, Aduro. An ancient curse is on its way to Avantia, and the Dark Wizard, Malvel is behind it. Thank goodness we have a hero, Tom, son of Taladon, to face such a threat. Read on to see if he will prevail!

PART ONE

THE DEADLY SWARM

THE DEADLY SWARM

Tom felt happy as he stared up at a sky full of stars. He was camping in the mountains with his father, Taladon, who was Avantia's Master of Beasts.

It was a humid night and as Tom wiped his forehead he felt something crawling on his skin. Brushing it off, he could see it was some kind of cockroach, its black shell gleaming in the moonlight. "Urgh!" he exclaimed, watching it fly away. Then Tom let out a gasp – the ground was crawling with insects, some creeping on the

sleeping Taladon. Tom jumped to his feet, waking his father.

"What are they?" Tom asked, as the stinking black-shelled creatures scuttled around his feet.

"I don't know," his father replied, puzzled, as the swarm skimmed close to their heads and was gone.

Something about the insects unsettled Tom, but after a few moments he and his father settled back down beside the fire. The smoke seemed to be moving...taking shape...

The Deadly Swarm

Tom's eyes widened. There was the face of his friend Elenna, who, together with her wolf, Silver, had accompanied him on his Quests. She looked worried.

"Avantia is suffering from an infestation of some kind of bug," she said. "The kingdom needs your help!"

At first light, Tom and Taladon galloped up to King Hugo's castle. Even though it was dawn, it already felt as hot as midday. Something was terribly wrong.

The stinking air was black with insects. As their horses, Storm and Fleetfoot, drank at a water trough, Tom noticed the castle walls were being eaten away by insects.

Tom banged on the door. A small window slid open and a pair of terrified eyes gazed out at them.

"The swarm," whispered the sentry, recognising Tom and Taladon. "It's eating everything it can find."

"Let us in!" Tom demanded. "We need to see King Hugo immediately."

Tom and Taladon raced up the stone steps and burst into the throne room where Aduro, the king's wizard, rose to greet them. Elenna was there too.

"Welcome," said King Hugo grimly, as Tom and Taladon watched precious tapestries being eaten by the bugs that swarmed over them.

"They are Stabiors," explained Elenna.

"But Stabiors left Avantia years ago!" Taladon said.

"Well, they're back," said Aduro soberly.

"Malvel," Tom guessed. "Is that who's done this?"

Everyone fell silent at the mention of the evil sorceror's name.

Creeaakk! They watched from the window as a huge tower, black with insects, crumbled to the ground before them.

Tom hurtled outside to the courtyard, where the rubble of the collapsed tower was settling. People limped past with gashes on their arms and legs.

"Captain Harkman has disappeared!" shouted a sentry, running through the dust. The captain was the commander of King Hugo's troops.

Tom shuddered. If the captain had been hit by the falling tower, it was almost certain that he was dead. As they searched through the rubble, clouds of Stabiors flew in black clouds.

Tom and Taladon hurried into the castle in case Harkman had taken refuge inside.

Rushing through the castle, Tom and Taladon eventually came up against a locked door.

"This is where the magical Golden Armour is kept!" Tom exclaimed. "Maybe the captain is in here!"

They rammed their shoulders at the door until

it broke from its hinges. There was no sign of Captain Harkman, but the Golden Armour had gone and the Master-of-Arms lay injured.

"The Stabiors," he gasped. "They carried pieces of the armour away. They crawled all over me! This breastplate is all that is left!"

"Malvel," said Taladon softly.

Tom felt a wave of anger break over him. "He won't get away with this," he vowed.

Back in the throne room, Tom noticed one of the magical tokens was glowing on his shield. It was Epos's talon. Epos was one of Avantia's six great Beasts – a huge phoenix who lived in the Stonewin volcano. She must need him.

As Tom explained to the king that he had to go, Aduro spoke. "Follow me," he said, leading Tom and Elenna to a secret room, deep beneath the castle.

Four suits of armour rested on stands. Tom reached out and touched the nearest breastplate.

"Stabiors!" he gasped, pulling his hand away.

"Stabior shells," said Aduro. "Woven into suits of armour. They resist and reflect heat," he explained. "I think you will find this armour useful on your Quest."

Tom and Elenna felt cool in their new armour, even as they galloped across the hot ground on Storm, with Elenna's wolf, Silver, running alongside. The Stonewin volcano was on the horizon, but it wasn't heat making it shimmer,

Tom realised. *It's a vast cloud of Stabiors!* As the ground became more difficult, they left the animals in the village of Rokwin, and continued on foot. The heat increased as they went higher. Their armour was the only thing keeping them alive. They walked quickly, the cloud of Stabiors and the outline of Epos the phoenix above them.

At the barren crown of the volcano, Epos lay on her side amongst a mass of smashed boulders.

"She's been injured." Elenna gasped. "There must have been a rockfall!"

Making their way quickly up the final stretch of the mountain path, Tom rushed to Epos's side. The phoenix's eyes were clouded with pain, and her plumage had lost its fiery colour.

At once, Tom and Elenna pulled away the rocks, the Stabiors buzzing madly around them, until with a mighty screech of joy, the phoenix raised both her wings and flew up into the sky.

Tom struggled up closer to the volcano to see that, instead of fire, broken rocks filled the crater. Those Stabiors that had survived the rockfall were busy eating away the edge of the crater. Tom realised they had blocked the volcano on purpose!

"No wonder the kingdom is warming up," said Elenna, standing beside him.

"The heat needs to escape somehow, or there's going to be..." said Tom slowly.

BOOOOM!

Tom and Elenna were thrown to the ground as boiling rocks rained down.

"The lava!" Tom gasped, lifting his head to watch a snake of red pour down the mountain, straight towards the village.

Tom jumped to his feet. They had to outpace the lava and warn the village, but the lava was so fast. He slid and scrambled down the mountainside. Elenna ran close beside him, her armour glittering. Epos wheeled and screeched overhead. Tom threw himself at a large rock and tried to push it into the path of the lava.

"If we can divert the flow, we can save Rokwin!" he shouted to Elenna. They pushed desperately, but they weren't strong enough. The boulder didn't move. "Get down to the village!" Tom said to Elenna. "Start evacuating the people! Everyone must leave!"

Who could Tom turn to for help? The answer came to him as he stared at the precious tokens on his shield. Arcta! The mountain giant. Of course!

Quickly, Tom rubbed the eagle feather that Arcta had given him, then scanned the horizon. First, he heard booming steps, then he saw Arcta's shaggy head rising above the mountains.

"Arcta!" Tom cried, delighted to see his old friend. "Throw!"

Arcta scooped up an armful of huge rocks and flung them into the lava. Slowly, the boiling river began to change direction. The people of Rokwin were safe.

The Deadly Swarm

Down in the village again, a thundercloud of Stabiors appeared from nowhere. Tom gazed up as the insects twisted and moved. Deep in their midst a face took shape – the face of Malvel.

"Until you meet Creta," echoed his booming voice, "you know nothing of the terror that awaits you."

Tom unsheathed his sword. "I've fought you before, Malvel, and I'll fight you again," he threatened bravely.

Malvel vanished, but the Stabiors re-formed into a vast column, sprouting arms and a terrifying face. A pair of huge orange eyes, with pupils like black lightning, gazed at Tom.

Tom knew this dreadful Beast was Creta.

As the giant Beast advanced, Tom saw that several pieces of the Golden Armour glinted on its limbs. He leapt back in shock as the creature leaned towards him and opened its mouth. A second face lurked inside Creta's mouth. It was a human face twisted in pain, with eyes full of terror.

It was Captain Harkman.

"Help!" the captain cried in desperation, as insects crawled across his face.

Tom suddenly realised what must have happened at the castle. Malvel's swarm had kidnapped the captain and trapped him inside this Beast. An unbeatable monster, made from the bodies of a hundred thousand insects.

POOR CAPTAIN HARKMAN – NOW AT THE mercy of Malvel's swarm. Have Tom and his faithful companions enough courage to overcome Creta and rescue the captain? Or will this be one challenge too many for Taladon's son?

PART TWO

WATER OF LIFE

WATER OF LIFE

STARING AT THE MONSTROUS BEAST THAT STOOD in front of him, Tom knew this would be a tough Quest. How could he fight a monster like Creta and save Captain Harkman? Arcta was still standing beside him in the village square, his gigantic feet planted like trees on either side of Rokwin's pond. He roared and swiped at Creta with fists like boulders, leaving a small hole in Creta's side. The Stabiors scattered to avoid the Beast's attack. Arcta's head disappeared in a cloud of black wings as he staggered from side to

Water of Life

side, while the hideous creatures clawed at his face.

"Distract him, Elenna!" Tom called, before watching with despair as the swarm slid away from her arrows and began to change shape. The Beast's front legs were now growing longer and more pointed. The tips divided and curled to form pincers that slashed the air. With his sword, Tom managed to shatter one. To his dismay, it immediately began to re-form. He threw himself towards the Beast again, whirling his sword to break up the swarm of Stabiors, and brushing them off his armour. He couldn't let them seize him in the way they had taken Captain Harkman.

Tom could feel the Stabiors marching up his neck, digging hard into his skin. They were in his hair and tickling his ears but he had no time to push them away because Creta's pincers were slashing all around him. Suddenly, Tom felt a stinging pain deep in his head. He dropped his sword and fell to his knees.

The voice, when it came, was icy cold as it boomed through Tom's head.

Now I have you!

Malvel's next words chilled Tom to the bone.

What can you do to defeat me, now that I am inside your head?

Tom shook his head. Malvel's laughter felt like poison.

"Look out!" Elenna screamed as, just in time, Tom rolled away from Creta's swarming pincer. He stumbled to his feet as a great shriek rang through the air. It was Epos, her magnificent red wings spread wide.

"Get back, Elenna!" Tom warned, as the phoenix's attack took Creta by surprise. As Epos's great wings tore through its body, Stabiors

were scattered in all directions. This time the swarm-Beast had no chance to rebuild itself. The buzzing black cloud broke apart and drifted back towards the village. Creta was defeated – for now.

Tom could feel Malvel's laughter fading, but he clutched his stomach as he felt a stabbing pain deep in his guts. He fell, and everything went black.

Opening his eyes much later, Tom found himself back at the castle, Elenna by his bedside. She must have brought him back somehow. All at once, memories rushed at Tom. He closed his eyes in shame as he remembered how Creta had defeated him.

Yes, Malvel hissed in his head. *You have failed, Tom.*

Tom pressed his hands against the sides of his head, trying to force the voice away.

"What is wrong with me, Elenna?" Tom asked.

"I can answer that," said a voice from a dark corner.

Tom hadn't noticed Marc sitting in the shadows, a book in his lap.

"I found this volume in Aduro's library," he said. "It mentions a plague similar to this one."

"How can the bugs be stopped?" asked Tom, feeling desperate.

"There is a spring high in the Shadow Mountains," Marc began. "Its water contains a powerful magic."

With an almighty effort, Tom swung his legs out of the bed. "Tell me how to get there," he said.

The young wizard stood up. "Before you begin this Quest, you need to know what's happened to you," he said grimly. "The Stabiors have laid their eggs inside you, Tom. If you don't drink some of the spring water yourself, you'll soon be under the Beast's control." Marc shook his head. "My magic will help you get there, but the rest is up to you."

Marc chanted a spell and the bedchamber began to swirl. When the mists cleared, Tom and Elenna found themselves in a strange, grey, foggy world, and in front of them was a giant waterfall crashing into a deep foaming pool.

Tom, groaning in pain, moved slowly towards the waterfall after Elenna. The fog was thickening and the waterall kept disappearing from view.

"I'll carry your shield," Elenna suggested, lifting it gently from Tom's back.

Suddenly, a foul smell hit Tom's senses.

Water of Life

Creta was back. Twisting round, Tom saw a great pincer rushing towards him, and rolled away just in time.

"Elenna," he croaked, as Creta lifted his evil head, black eyes looming.

Suddenly Creta stumbled, and split in half as Elenna flung Tom's shield at the monster. The Stabiors swarmed, then flew away among the rocks.

Tom crawled towards his shield and fastened it safely onto his back. "Creta will return," he said. "We have to keep going."

The waterfall and its pool taunted them, flickering in and out of sight in the mist.

The next time Creta appeared, Tom was ready.

He slammed his shield into Creta's chest, the only part unprotected by the Golden Armour. Creta roared with pain as one huge foot entered the foaming river. A glint of hope surged through Tom. "If we can get the Beast into the pool, the battle will be won," he shouted to Elenna.

Tom was in such pain now, he was crawling along on his knees. For safety, they stayed close to the river, as Creta was keeping a wary distance from its glittering depths.

Just ahead of him, Tom watched as Elenna slipped and fell into a marshy pool. The water sucked hungrily at her as she struggled.

"Don't," Tom mumbled. "Struggling makes it worse..."

Panting, he crawled closer and Elenna seized his hand. Despite the pain, Tom dragged her free, Stabiors dive-bombing them from all directions.

"We're nearly there, Tom," Elenna said to him.

"Then you must drink."

Courage pushed him onwards.

As the spray of the waterfall touched Tom's face, he lifted his head and opened his eyes. He crawled to a ledge at the very base of the falls as Stabiors swarmed overhead, afraid to come too close to the water. Tom pulled himself onto the ledge and let the water pound down on him. He rolled onto his back and opened his mouth. Tom felt the water's cleansing power as Malvel screamed from within him in fury. As magic coursed through Tom's body, the pain and burning ceased. The curse was gone.

Tom sprang to his feet, feeling more alive than he could ever remember. Down by the edge of

the pool, he could see Elenna fighting off the Stabiors. Creta prowled around the far side of the pool, grunting with rage. Tom saw he could come no closer. The waterfall spray burned him like fire. He thrust his sword into the cascading water, then jumped down from the ledge.

His sword dripped magical water. Striding towards Creta, Tom taunted the Beast.

"Scared of water, are you?" he said.

Creta moved like lightning, his pincers crashing towards Tom.

Tom quickly darted out of the way, magical water dripping from his sword.

Jabbing wildly at the Beast, at last Tom felt his sword connect with the Stabiors. Bugs rained down,

hissing gently as the water burned them away to nothing. Elenna cheered as Creta staggered. One of his pincers had broken into pieces. Tom dropped down and dipped his sword in the water again.

"Look out, Tom!" Elenna screamed suddenly.

Whirling round, Tom stabbed instinctively with his sword. Creta the Winged Terror was right behind him, but now he was staggering again.

This time Tom stabbed the Beast through the middle.

The tottering Beast keeled over and fell into the pool. There was a flash of white fire as Creta disappeared beneath the water and a great geyser erupted, shooting skywards. Tom and Elenna both heard a shriek coming from deep beneath the pool's glittering surface before the water settled to stillness. It was the voice of Malvel.

Tom hardly dared hope that they had won.

"They've gone!" Elenna said into the silence.

Tom stepped back as something bubbled and exploded to the surface. It was Captain Harkman, coughing and spluttering, but alive... and wearing the Golden Armour.

"Well done, Tom and Elenna!" came a familiar voice.

Aduro stood smiling on the banks of the pool in a shimmering ring of fire.

"What news of the castle?" asked Elenna anxiously.

"The creatures have gone," said Aduro. "And the king awaits you!"

The wizard waved his wand and they were magically whisked back to the castle. Happy faces met Tom and Elenna everywhere they looked.

"I thank you," said King Hugo warmly, "for driving this fresh peril from our kingdom. Thanks to you, and to young Marc's magic, we are safe again. Let the feasting and celebrating begin!"

Water of Life

Arax
The Soul Stealer

MY MASTER, THE GOOD WIZARD, ADURO, is in danger. The Dark Wizard, Malvel, has cast a powerful spell on him. Brave Tom now faces his greatest challenge yet. Can he save his friend Aduro and protect the kingdom of Avantia? Read on to see!

PART ONE

A FRIEND LOST

A FRIEND LOST

TOM AND ELENNA WERE STAYING AT THE palace as guests of King Hugo. Sunshine streamed through the windows as the friends ran downstairs. Then Tom stopped. "What can you hear, Elenna?" he asked.

"Nothing," she replied. "It's really quiet."

"Exactly," said Tom. "We haven't even seen a servant."

The Great Hall lay silent. The king's throne was empty. No fire had been lit.

"It's really spooky," agreed Elenna.

Then a guard burst in.

"You there," he said. "I have orders from the king. You must go to the wizard Aduro's chambers straight away."

"Where is everyone?" asked Elenna.

"They are in their rooms, by order of the king. The palace is not safe," replied the guard.

Tom and Elenna ran up the spiral staircase that led to Aduro's private rooms. The wooden door glowed strangely around the edges.

Inside, the friends found a man with wild eyes, hissing and growling. He was being closely watched by guards.

The man was their old friend, the Good Wizard Aduro himself.

Tom stared in horror. Aduro's face, usually filled with kindness, was instead twisted in anger.

Suddenly, the old wizard leapt up, jabbing Tom with his finger.

"Evil Malvel must have done this to Aduro!" Tom said.

Marc, the apprentice, muttered some words and

A Friend Lost

an image of a giant creature formed in the air. It had a horned head and wings like a bat. It was hitting Aduro with a whip of thorns which tore into his heart. Aduro cried out and a look of evil replaced the kindness in his eyes.

As the vision disappeared, King Hugo said sadly, "The Beast has stolen Aduro's soul, and left this behind." The king showed them a scrap of material stained with blood.

"My name is sewn into it!" Tom said, frightened.

King Hugo stared into Tom's eyes. "I am going to send you on a Quest. You will need to be strong and brave. Malvel's new Beast must be found before more damage is caused to our kingdom."

"You can count on me," declared Tom. Elenna agreed.

"Take great care and fight bravely. Avantia depends on you," finished the king.

As they ran off, Tom heard a whisper in his head. *Arax the Soul Stealer will find you!* it said. The voice was Malvel's.

Tom and Elenna ran to the stables to find their faithful friends. Tom unlatched the door and saddled Storm, his black stallion, ready for the journey. Meanwhile Silver, Elenna's pet wolf, dashed around, barking with excitement.

"Where do we find this new Beast?" asked Elenna. "He could be anywhere."

"My map will tell us," said Tom. He began to open it and then suddenly stopped. He looked worried. "Aduro gave this map to me," he said.

"Will it be any use to us, without his Good Magic?"

"There's only one way to find out," Elenna told him.

Together, they unrolled the map and laid it out. The parchment looked blank. Then, to Tom's relief, a picture of Avantia appeared. "Yes!" he exclaimed. "The map's magic is still working."

"Then it must show Arax," said Elenna, kneeling at his side.

"Look!" cried Tom suddenly. "That's him!"

The two friends watched the tiny shape of Arax circle the mountaintops, then swoop down and vanish into the rock.

"We should have guessed that's where he'd be," said Elenna. "Arax is a bat – and bats live in caves!"

"Let's go!" said Tom, scrambling to his feet.

Tom leapt onto Storm's back and Elenna jumped up behind him. Soon they were out of the city and heading west, with the brave wolf Silver bounding along beside them.

A Friend Lost

They rode for hours and by late afternoon the flat ground had given way to rocky slopes. They could see the mountains in the distance.

Storm had dropped to a slow trot, the loose rocks slippery under his hooves.

Tom could hear a faint rushing sound. "We must have reached Winding River!" he said. "Let's set up camp here."

After a meal of berries and bread, they lay down to sleep.

Tom opened his eyes next morning to blue skies and warm sun. "Breakfast is served," joked Elenna, passing him a handful of nuts and berries.

When they had eaten, Tom got out his map and scanned the tall peaks. A tiny dark shape appeared on the map and then vanished again into a hole in the side of a mountain.

"That must be Arax's cave!" said Elenna. "But how do we get to it?"

"There must be a path," replied Tom, jumping up into Storm's saddle. "Come on!" Elenna leapt up behind him.

It wasn't long before they reached the start of the trail, the mountain peaks high above them. Silver followed Storm closely as the stallion picked his way over the sharp rocks of the narrow path. The route soon became steep.

A Friend Lost

"We're climbing fast," said Elenna. "It's colder already."

Eventually the path became so difficult for Storm that Tom and Elenna jumped from the saddle. The four friends slowly struggled up the path together.

The sky was getting darker as they listened to the stream pounding over the rocks and great flocks of birds swooping and calling around the mountain tops.

"It's spooky here," muttered Elenna. "Do you think we're getting close to Arax's cave?"

Tom looked around at the bare grey rock dotted with scrubby bushes. "There's a dark cave there," he exclaimed. "Just like the one on the map!"

As they struggled towards the mouth of the cave, Elenna stopped. "I saw something!" she said with a gasp.

A horrible hissing sound filled the air, and before Tom could do anything, a long whip shot out of the cave and wrapped itself around Elenna.

A Friend Lost

Tom jumped towards her, but it was too late.

Elenna was dragged into the dark cave and disappeared among the shadows.

Tom recognised the whip from the vision Marc had shown them. Arax had taken Elenna! "Stay here," he ordered the animals, as he crept into the cave. Where could Elenna be?

Inside the cave, the air was suddenly filled with high-pitched squeaks. A cloud of bats whirled around Tom. He tried to swipe at the creatures with his sword but there were too many of them. Their clawed feet scratched his face and their wings slapped against his skin.

The shrieking bats swooped and dived. At last they tore out of the cave and Tom was alone again. He had to find Elenna. After a while, Tom realised he could hear the sound of running water. His heart was pounding as at last he came

across a huge waterfall stretching across his path. He took a deep breath and plunged in, taking careful steps until he was through.

Tom's face streamed with water but when his vision cleared, he saw Elenna, her face pale. A creature with huge claws grasped her around the throat. It was Arax!

A Friend Lost

The Beast took hold of the spiked whip in one clawed hand. Tom felt sick knowing that the giant bat's whip could strike him at any time. He could see that Elenna was not hurt. Arax had been using her as bait to lure him into the cave.

As Tom charged forward the Beast was distracted for a few seconds and Elenna just managed to pull herself free. Arax flew at Tom, swirling his whip around. Faster and faster it went until, with an almighty crack, it ripped through his tunic. Tom cried out as the spikes bit into his flesh, their poison going deep.

The giant bat pulled the whip back and began to whirl it around again. As the evil whip twisted, a shadowy figure began to appear, which grew bigger. Then the bat-Beast, Arax, shrieked in triumph and vanished into the cave leaving the shadowy figure in front of Tom and Elenna. They gazed at the figure as it became more solid. It wasn't a huge Beast. It was only a boy who looked just like Tom.

"He looks like me," said Tom.

"No, his eyes are nothing like yours," said Elenna. "They're pure evil."

"My name is Nemico," snarled the boy. "You've met your match at last."

A Friend Lost

ONCE ADURO FELT THE BITE OF ARAX'S whip, his soul was taken. Now he is a danger to himself and to Avantia. Can Tom and Elenna defeat the Beast, or will they meet the same terrible fate?

PART TWO

RETURN OF A HERO

RETURN OF A HERO

"We're the same," Nemico told Tom. "But one fights for Good, and the other for Evil!"

Elenna took her chance and slipped safely out of the cave.

Desperate to follow her, Tom sliced his sword down through the air towards Nemico again and again until, at last, he drove the boy out onto the narrow mountain path. As Tom lunged hard with his sword, an arrow from Elenna flew past Nemico's head.

"Foolish girl," Nemico muttered. He took his shield and sent it spinning through the air, straight at her head.

The shield slammed into Elenna's head with a horrible thud, and she collapsed.

"Elenna!" Tom gasped. "Are you all right?"

As his friend slowly got to her feet, Tom felt sick with relief.

"He won't beat us," Elenna told him. Stumbling up onto a flat rock, brave Elenna released arrow after arrow towards Nemico. But the boy caught each one as it fell. Tom thought he saw despair in Elenna's eyes. They could not do this alone. Tom felt his own determined spirit being drained by Arax's poisoned whip. He would need to call upon one of Avantia's Good Beasts to help.

Tom raised his sword over his head. "Ferno the Fire Dragon!" he shouted. "I call on you now!"

Nemico ran towards Tom. "Why don't you just give in?" he mocked, jabbing at Tom with his sword.

"While there's blood in my veins, you won't defeat me," Tom told his enemy.

He felt so weak now, and Nemico was strong. It took all of Tom's remaining energy to fight him.

At last, Tom heard the sound of huge wings beating the air. It was the Good Beast, Ferno, and he had come to help.

Tom gazed up at Ferno. The dragon dived at the evil boy, surrounding him with flames. Nemico crouched down, using his leather shield

as protection until it melted away.

Shocked, he took a few steps backwards, away from the heat, but he was on the very edge of the narrow path. As Nemico teetered on the

edge, Tom saw the fear on his face. Even though this boy was his deadly enemy, Tom dived forwards and made a grab for his hand.

Return of a Hero

But it was too late. With a howl of despair, Tom's evil double fell over the edge.

Tom looked down. The drop made him feel dizzy, but somehow Nemico was hanging just below the ledge, clinging on by his fingers.

"Help!" Nemico whispered. "Help me...please."

"Let him fall, Tom," he heard Elenna say. Ferno circled above them, snorting in agreement.

But Tom knew he couldn't let Nemico die. He reached out to grasp the boy's sleeve.

Nemico smiled up at Tom, but for once his eyes didn't have their usual evil glint. His hand slipped through Tom's as if it wasn't there, and he vanished in a cloud of smoke.

"What's happening?" Tom gasped as the smoke

whirled around him. Gradually, the clouds became a thin spiral that shot into his body through the wound left by Arax's whip.

Return of a Hero

At first Tom felt as if his heart was going to burst, but then he felt...wonderful! His old feelings of strength and determination were returning.

"Tom!" said Elenna, running up to him. "Are you all right?"

"I'm fine," Tom told her. "Everything Arax stole from me has come back. Something must have happened when I took Nemico's hand. I made the right choice when I tried to save him."

A shriek came from the air above Tom and Elenna. They could feel the beating of huge wings as the giant bat flew right over their heads.

"Watch out!" yelled Elenna, as the Beast swooped towards Tom.

Whoosh! Ferno came diving down towards

Arax, unleashing a blast of fire. But Arax was not defeated. He still had his whip, which he flicked straight at Ferno. The fire dragon bellowed and took to the air, avoiding Arax's evil barbs.

"Thank you for helping us, Ferno," Tom shouted up into the air. "It's up to me now. I must finish this Quest!"

With his power restored, Tom knew he was ready for anything. Ferno seemed to understand, and flew away. With his weapons ready, Tom turned to face his enemy.

Slowly, the Beast began to advance, flicking his long whip. Just as Arax reached him, Tom swung his shield up. It clashed with the Beast's horns and one horn sank deep into the shield.

Return of a Hero

Arax shrieked madly, trying to shake it free.

"For Aduro!" Tom yelled. He brought his sword

down on the other horn and sliced it off.

Arax stumbled about wildly. He managed to shake off the shield but there was no time for Tom to pick it up.

I know the best place to be to avoid Arax's whip, Tom thought, as he jumped onto a rock and leapt high in the air towards Arax's back.

The giant bat snarled with rage as he tried and failed to use his whip against Tom.

Tom raised his sword, but Arax wasn't beaten yet. As the Beast took flight, Tom felt a great lurch. He could do nothing but cling on tightly as Arax sped through the mountain air.

Higher and higher Tom and Arax flew. Tom could see Elenna far below.

The air around them grew icy cold as the bat-Beast swooped this way and that, until finally Arax shot upwards into the thick grey cloud with Tom on his back.

Swiftly, Tom raised his sword and struck Arax hard over the head. The giant bat cried out in pain and dropped from the sky.

Crash! Arax and Tom fell heavily onto a mountain ledge. The landing was hard and Tom could hardly breathe. Through his pain, he heard Elenna running towards him.

"Tom! Are you all right?" she cried desperately.

"Don't worry," Tom called back. He knew he'd been lucky. Arax had taken the force of the fall. But Tom could feel the Beast begin to heave himself up beneath him.

Tom desperately tried to scramble away but he was caught in the giant bat's wings. Then he heard a noise that terrified him. Arax's whip was slicing through the air. The Beast might be hurt, but he was still lashing out.

Return of a Hero

With all his strength, Tom pushed out his arms and kicked with his legs. The sudden movement knocked Arax off balance, and the whip was flung from the Beast's claws.

Desperately, Tom threw his head to one side to avoid the whip. The leather cord snaked past him and sank its spikes into the Beast's own heart. With a roar of despair, Arax flung his wings wide – Tom was free! The Beast let out a wail of fear and pain as he tried to pull the whip from his chest.

Elenna ran to Tom's side and they watched as a cloud of smoke burst from Arax's chest. The smoke twisted and turned then broke apart into thin strands, glowing with every colour of the rainbow.

"They must be all the souls Arax has stolen," whispered Tom, as the strands blew away.

"Do you think the souls are going back to their owners?" asked Elenna.

Tom nodded. "I'm counting on it if Aduro is to be saved," he said.

Tom ran to find his sword and shield from among the rocks, and strode forwards. "Now it's time to finish off this Evil Beast for ever," he said.

But something was happening. All over his body, Arax's leathery skin was curling up like paper in a fire. He was turning into dust before Tom and Elenna's astonished eyes!

A sudden wind blew up, whipping the dust.

It was swept into a whirlwind. Tom thought he heard a faint cry of fury as the cloud was blown high over the tops of the mountains.

Return of a Hero

"You did it, Tom!" yelled Elenna. "You defeated Arax!"

"I've never been so happy to be alive!" Tom said, smiling.

They climbed down the path to where Silver and Storm were waiting patiently. The stallion gave a whinny of welcome. Then the air shimmered and a vision of Aduro appeared.

"I thank you both, Tom and Elenna," the Good Wizard said. "You have rescued me from a terrible torment."

Tom looked hard at the vision of the wizard. "You seem very tired," he said. "Will you recover?"

"In time," Aduro replied. His face was still pale, but he smiled. He raised his staff to Tom and Elenna. "Farewell!"

And he was gone.

"Let's go back to the palace for breakfast!" said Tom happily.

Silver ran along barking in delight and Storm trotted ahead. Tom looked at his friend and smiled. How could he ever fail with such companions at his side?

He raised his sword to the sky. "To our next Quest!" Tom cried.

Mortaxe
The Skeleton Warrior

I'M TOM'S FRIEND, ELENNA. IT HAS BEEN AN honour for Silver and me to join Tom on his Quests – together we have never failed. But our enemies do not rest. Keep reading, if you think your heart is as strong as mine.

PART ONE

THE CALM BEFORE THE STORM

THE CALM BEFORE THE STORM

TOM SIGHED AS HE PULLED ON HIS ROBE AND looked down at his feet in their sparkling slippers. He didn't feel very comfortable, but King Hugo was throwing a party, and Tom was a guest at the palace. The clothes had been left in his bedchamber, and a servant had asked him to try the outfit on.

Suddenly, Tom's door flew open. It was Elenna.

"Just look what they've done to me!" she said angrily.

His good friend wore a shimmering yellow

dress and had a tiara plonked on top of her short, spiky hair. Tom tried hard not to giggle.

Suddenly, there was a loud bang outside and Tom rushed to the window. As Tom looked around, there came another loud noise, but this time an orange light burst above the turrets like a firework.

The Calm Before the Storm

"Look!" said Elenna, pointing.

Aduro was standing on a patch of bare ground.

"He must be preparing fireworks for the celebrations!" Tom laughed.

Whistling loudly, Tom managed to get the Good Wizard's attention, just as yet another explosion rattled the windows and shook the walls.

Tom frowned. This was not a firework display. This was something else. Something bad.

As smoke rose into the sky, Aduro began to run.

"Go and change," said Tom, tearing off the grand robes and grabbing his shield and sword. "I'll meet you downstairs."

A short while later, Tom and Elenna hurried towards the site of the explosion.

The smoke had almost cleared when they caught up with the Good Wizard in a far corner of the dark stables. They watched as he threw hay bales aside, revealing a trapdoor.

The Calm Before the Storm

Aduro tapped the door with his staff. It creaked open to reveal stone steps.

"These lead to the Gallery of Tombs," he explained. "The explosion was down there."

Tom looked at Elenna in surprise. He had no idea this place existed.

Aduro led the way down the stairs into the dark until, at last, they reached the bottom. Walking one behind the other, they followed a narrow passage. Thick cobwebs hung from the mossy walls.

As the tunnel widened, Tom could see stone caskets standing up against the walls.

"This place must be hundreds of years old," Elenna muttered.

"The Gallery of Tombs is older than the castle itself," said Aduro quietly. "Every Master of Beasts is buried here. If the Gallery has been disturbed then Evil must be close by."

Exploring further, they came across two caskets

laid in front of them. Tom read the letters on the first. TANNER, FIRST MASTER OF THE BEASTS.

The tomb beside Tanner's read simply MORTAXE.

Before Tom could ask Aduro about the tombs, a beam of light exploded from the shadows, knocking him backwards.

Another beam hit Aduro, pinning him to the ground.

"Come closer and I'll snap his bones like twigs," came a girl's sneering voice. In the semi-darkness Tom made out the figure of a girl with glowing eyes.

"You don't look much like a hero," said the ghostly figure to Tom. "But then Malvel always did call you an annoying little runt."

Malvel. Tom should have known he would be behind this.

"I am Petra," the girl continued. "And together,

Malvel and I are going to take over the whole of Avantia."

Tom felt his anger burn as he charged at her.

A look of fury crossed Petra's face as she lifted her arm to fire another bolt of light at him.

Tom brought up his sword as the fierce power brought rocks tumbling down around him.

"Did you really think it would be that easy?" Petra said, as she sprang off the ground and hovered high up in the chamber, looking down at Tom.

"Come down here and fight!" Tom demanded.

Petra sneered as a beam fired from her finger into the tomb of Mortaxe. As Tom watched in horror, something like molten metal spread over the tomb's surface. The stone caved in, revealing a black space within.

"Arise, Mortaxe," Petra said in a whisper.

Tom watched in horror as five fingers crept over the edge of the tomb. He took a step back.

Something Evil had arrived.

Mortaxe was like no Beast Tom had ever seen before. He looked like a human skeleton, but was more than twice the height of the tallest

person Tom had ever met. The terrifying creature faced Tom, glaring at him with empty eyes that glowed red.

Mortaxe climbed out of the tomb. Tom stared at the Beast's chest, where a heart the size of a human head was beating. Tom looked over in panic at Aduro, still trapped by Petra.

"Welcome back, Mortaxe!" Petra called out. "Your time has come again!"

The Beast grabbed a weapon from his tomb. Tom leapt forwards and blocked the blow as it came. Mortaxe roared, hurling Tom aside. Elenna shot an arrow towards Petra. The evil girl lost concentration and the beam of energy keeping Aduro captive fell. The wizard was free.

He stood up dizzily and spread his arms. In each hand a ball of light appeared. He sent them spinning towards Petra. There was a crash as she shot her own light back.

"You will not defeat us," Petra said fiercely.

Petra soared down to the chamber floor and

scurried into the shadows. Tom and Elenna charged at Mortaxe. The Beast bellowed with rage as he slashed with his weapon. As Tom ducked, he felt the blade slice through his hair. He leapt forwards and stabbed at the Beast's heart, but Mortaxe turned.

Tom's blade was caught between his ribs.

"Stand back!" called Aduro suddenly. As Tom leapt away, the wizard hurled a spinning orb of light towards Mortaxe. But the Beast swept the ball aside, and rushed away with his evil partner, Petra.

Catching his breath, Aduro began to explain. "Mortaxe was once a brave soldier called Tarik. He fought alongside Tanner, but fell victim to the spell of an Evil Wizard. Tarik's good heart was still strong so the wizard swapped it for the heart of a cursed bull Beast. Now Mortaxe has the power to turn all Beasts to his evil will."

Aduro urged Tom to prise an etched map from the top of Tanner's tomb. As Tom held it up, his

shield began to vibrate and his brain was filled with the bellows of distressed Beasts.

"Something terrible is happening," he said.

Tom heard Aduro's voice close to his ear. "Mortaxe's will has touched the Beasts already."

"We must go," said Tom, as he and Elenna raced back along the passage and out into the stables. They both jumped onto Storm's back as Elenna whistled for Silver.

Tom checked the map and saw a tiny Mortaxe moving towards the Central Plains.

Shriek!

Soaring through the air above them was Epos the Flame Bird. She turned into a steep dive and Tom was shocked to see the fireball between her talons.

"Look out," he said. "She's going to attack!"

Epos hurled the fireball towards them. Tom just managed to steer Storm away from its burning path.

"Epos is a Good Beast," cried Tom. "But Mortaxe has already used his wicked powers to make her evil."

They rode on, leaving the great creature circling above. At last they came to the Central Plains, where Mortaxe should have been, but all was empty and silent.

"Where is he?" asked Elenna, looking across the endless land.

Before Tom could answer, they heard a deep groan from a patch of ground ahead. A crack opened up and from it rose a wall of stone.

The wall grew into a vast circle all around them. Six arches appeared in the sides, with long benches made of stone.

"It's an arena!" whispered Elenna.

The ground shook further as a huge carved chair emerged. Mortaxe was sitting in it, gripping his weapon and now wearing chest armour. Petra was standing close by.

"Look!" said Tom, pointing at the six arches. Elenna gasped as she made out the six Good Beasts of Avantia. Normally the sight of the

The Calm Before the Storm

Beasts filled Tom with wonder. Now there was only anger. How dare anyone poison their noble hearts with evil magic?

TOM AND I ARE MARCHING RIGHT INTO the heart of the battle between Avantia's Good Beasts. But how can my friend possibly survive a battle against a Skeleton Warrior who has such immense power over the Good Beasts?

PART TWO

BATTLE OF THE BEASTS

BATTLE OF THE BEASTS

THE BEASTS ROARED TOGETHER, BLASTING anger and hatred.

"This place is for combat," said Tom. "The Beasts are going to be made to fight each other."

Running towards them, Tom saw that he was right. Ferno and Nanook faced each other.

Ferno reared back and fire shot from his mouth. The snow monster bellowed and Tom could smell burning fur.

Nanook stamped towards Ferno, gripping one wing to pull the dragon off balance.

Battle of the Beasts

"Don't hurt each other!" Tom called desperately.

Suddenly Ferno swept down, as Sepron wrapped his long neck around Nanook's leg.

As Tom tried to help Nanook, Tagus the Horse-Man charged, battering them with his hooves. Moments later, Arcta the Mountain Giant was set upon by Ferno and knocked to the ground.

Tom looked round for Elenna. He desperately needed her help. But as he locked eyes with her, he heard her speak to Ferno. The words chilled his very bones.

"That's right!" said his once loyal friend. "Kill him!"

"You have to help me!" he said.

Elenna grinned. "From now on, I only help myself," she said coldly.

Tom couldn't believe what he was hearing.

Could Mortaxe's magic really be so strong?

Mortaxe was laughing, but there was worse. Silver and Storm were at the foot of the skeleton warrior's throne. Suddenly, Storm kicked Silver hard, sending him flying across the arena. Tom gasped. They too had been bewitched.

Tom's gaze returned to the fight. Ferno had broken away from Arcta and had now been joined in the sky by Epos the Flame Bird. The two Beasts dived at one another, blasting jets of fire. They clashed and fell in a tangled heap of burning feathers.

Tom looked around with anger. Six Good Beasts were suffering. It was time to end this.

He held his sword high.

"You won't get away with this!" Tom shouted to Petra. "While there's blood in my veins. . ."

"Don't you ever get bored of saying that?" Elenna laughed cruelly.

Mortaxe

Tom turned as he heard a great thudding noise coming closer. It was Mortaxe.

"This arena was built for death, and death there will be," Petra spat.

Mortaxe stood in the centre of the arena. He towered over Tom. His eyes showed no pity. Tom had no doubt this would be a duel to the death, and he knew he was completely on his own.

As Tom gripped his shield, he saw the Beasts return to their arches. Several were bleeding and in pain.

As the sky darkened and lightning flashed across the sky, the evil Mortaxe turned his skull upwards. Tom saw his chance. He rushed forward and struck at the Beast with his sword.

The Evil Beast yelled and slashed with his weapon, knocking Tom off his feet. As Tom struggled to get up, he came face to face with Storm. The stallion rushed at Tom, thrusting

with his head. Tom cried out as he was pushed backwards.

Mortaxe peered down at Tom, as the Beasts of Avantia roared and screeched in excitement.

The skeleton warrior's weapon crashed down again. Tom managed to roll aside and scramble up.

Tom drove his sword into Mortaxe's knee. It seemed to be made of stone. How could Tom fight a Beast that was already dead?

Tom suddenly knew what he had to do. Mortaxe may have been a skeleton, but his heart was still alive. His heart was the part given to the Beast by the Evil Wizard. This was the key to Mortaxe's power, but Tom couldn't do it alone.

Elenna was watching with an arrow in her bow. Tom could see it tracking him as he moved around.

Mortaxe raised his weapon and lunged, just as Tom tried to drive his sword through the thick leather of the Beast's breastplate. Tom was aiming for the heart. Mortaxe was enraged and came at Tom again.

Tom felt real fear. Even if he managed to get to the heart and defeat the Beast, Petra was waiting with her magic and Elenna was ready with an arrow. Then there would still be Storm, Silver and six angry Beasts to face.

Tom knew Elenna was still watching him. She wouldn't hesitate to fire her arrow.

Battle of the Beasts

Maybe there is a way to get Elenna's help, even if she doesn't want to give it, he thought.

Tom pretended to fall and Mortaxe did as he had hoped. The Beast reached out with a bony hand and gripped Tom by the throat, holding him up in the air for all to see.

"You always got in the way," Tom croaked to Elenna. "The Quests would have been much easier if you'd just stayed at home."

Elenna's face went white with rage. She fired her arrow directly at him.

Tom jerked his body upwards, breaking Mortaxe's grip and feeling the arrow swish past him. As Tom fell to the ground, he looked up and saw the arrow buried deep in the Beast's eye socket.

"Got you!" he shouted.

The skeleton warrior roared and staggered. He swung his weapon wildly and Tom watched as the Beast sliced through his own chest armour, revealing his heart.

Before Tom had a chance to work out what to do next, the Beast used his free hand to tug the arrow from his eye and snap it.

As Tom staggered against a wall, the furious Beast took mighty steps towards him. Tom managed to turn aside at the last minute and Mortaxe brought his weapon down into solid stone. At once, Tom gripped his sword and turned to the distracted Beast.

"My turn!" he shouted.

Tom brought down the blade on Mortaxe's arm. He sliced it clean off.

Mortaxe gave a roar of anger. Tom reached for the wooden handle of the Beast's weapon and, with a grunt of effort, pulled it free from the stone.

Battle of the Beasts

"Enough!" screamed Petra. "Kill him, Mortaxe!"

Tom glanced up and could see Malvel's evil apprentice high above. A wicked light shone in Petra's eyes as she rubbed her hands.

"I don't think so," Tom muttered under his breath.

It took all Tom's strength to lift the Beast's weapon. With a yell, he heaved it across Mortaxe's chest, finally exposing the Beast's heart.

Around the edges of the arena, the once Good and brave Beasts of Avantia roared and screeched in anger. Storm and Silver growled and kicked at the ground nearby. Everyone was against Tom.

With his hands, Tom reached into the skeleton warrior's chest and grasped the Beast's evil heart.

Tom pulled it free.

The Beast's mouth fell open. No sound came out. Then, incredibly, Mortaxe's bones began to fall apart before Tom's eyes.

Any life there had been within Mortaxe's deep eye sockets was gone.

"No!" screamed Petra. "It can't be!"

Tom threw the heart aside. A huge shadow fell

over him. The Beasts were approaching.

"I don't want to fight you," Tom said to them desperately.

The huge creatures formed a semi-circle around Tom. He picked up his sword, but he knew he couldn't hold off six Beasts.

With a screech, Epos suddenly hurled a fireball, but not at Tom. It crashed into the arena wall, making the whole place shake and creating a great hole. Rocks tumbled to the ground. Tom waited for one of the creatures to attack. But it didn't happen. Instead, one by one, the Good Beasts moved away from him.

Tagus kicked away chunks of stone. Arcta pushed against a wall until it crumbled and fell.

The Beasts were destroying the arena! Tom couldn't help the smile that spread across his face. Mortaxe's spell was broken!

"What are you doing?" Petra shouted to them.

The Beasts on the ground continued to heave the great stones away. Above, Ferno swooped towards the evil witch, breathing fire. In a cloud of smoke, Petra vanished.

As the smoke cleared, Tom caught sight of Elenna lying on the ground. Her skin was pale and her eyes closed.

The air was thick with smoke and the whole ground seemed to shake like an earthquake. Tom carried his friend from the now burning and crumbling arena. They collapsed on the soft grass

outside. Rolling over, Tom saw the Beasts escaping to safety after them.

Elenna's eyelids flickered, then opened.

"What happened? I don't remember anything," she said, putting out her hand to stroke her faithful wolf, Silver, now gentle and calm once more.

"Tom, did we argue?" she asked, confused. "I seem to remember we did."

"I don't know what you're talking about," he said smiling. "When do we ever argue?"

Ravira

Ruler of the Underworld

MY NOSTRILS FLARE AS I SEND OUT A HOWL. Fear spreads through the kingdom. The time has come. Humans, fear us. Heroes, tremble. The Hounds of Avantia have been unleashed! Read on if you dare!

PART ONE

THE HOUNDS OF AVANTIA

THE HOUNDS OF AVANTIA

Tom was in his chamber at King Hugo's palace one sunny morning, when Aduro burst in.

"Terrible news!" he said, panting. "Your father, Taladon, is in danger! There has been a disturbance in the village of Shrayton," he went on.

"What kind of disturbance?" Tom asked the Good Wizard.

"A terrible evil," muttered Aduro. "A cursed Beast – Ravira."

Tom suddenly felt the chill of fear.

"Ravira is the most cruel Beast ever to stalk this kingdom," said Aduro. "But she is supposed to stay in the underworld. Your father was bitten by one of her servants – a Hound of Avantia."

"Is my father dead?" asked Tom, quietly.

"He lives," replied Aduro. "But in the light of tonight's moon, he will change and become a Hound of Avantia too. He will then be cursed to live for eternity as a vicious dog, serving the Beast, Ravira."

Suddenly, Tom's friend, Elenna, was at the door. She had heard their anxious voices.

"We must go at once," called Tom, darting from the room with Elenna close behind.

They headed to the stables to saddle up Tom's faithful stallion, Storm, and were on their way. Elenna's loyal wolf, Silver, ran alongside them.

Storm's powerful legs carried them towards Shrayton. After many hours, they burst onto a

muddy track marked with other hoofprints.

"This must be the way," said Elenna.

After a while, a shape appeared far in the distance. Tom let Storm slow his pace and saw that it was a boy.

"Are you Tom?" asked the boy. "Taladon told me to expect a boy and a girl on a black horse. I'm Jacob."

Tom jumped down from the saddle. They had arrived. "Where is my father?" he asked.

"Follow me," said Jacob, leading the way towards a stable.

"Quick!" Jacob hissed, hurrying them around the side. Towards the village, they watched a crowd carrying weapons and flaming torches gathering.

"They patrol the streets looking for people who've been bitten," said Jacob. "They don't know your father is here."

As the boy pushed the stable door open, Tom saw Taladon inside. His wrists were in chains.

"Why have you locked him up?" he asked angrily.

Before the boy could answer, Tom's father sprang from the ground, his face twisted with rage.

As Tom jumped back in shock, he saw that thick hair coated the back of Taladon's neck.

"What's happened to you?" Tom asked.

"You shouldn't have come," Taladon croaked. "It's too late."

Tom saw that his father's eyes looked like those of a wild animal.

"I did as he asked," Jacob muttered.

"He insisted that I lock him up. He'd seen what happened to the others when they were bitten."

Tom and Elenna looked at him in confusion.

"The next night," Jacob went on, "when the moon rises, they turn into Hounds."

"We have to fight Ravira," Tom said. "Where is her lair?"

Taladon's reply was lost in a gruesome howl as he began to transform before their eyes.

"Come on, Tom!" cried Elenna. "He can't help us now!"

As they left the stable, Jacob locked the door. Glancing towards Silver, he whispered, "I think I know the way to Ravira, but you should leave the wolf here. Your horse, too."

Tom didn't like the idea of leaving his companions, but at least they would be staying with his father.

Jacob picked up Taladon's sword and passed it to Tom.

"You should take this," Tom said, handing it to Elenna.

As they made their way towards the centre of Shrayton, Tom felt uneasy.

"Taladon is a great fighter." Tom frowned. "How did one of these Hounds get close enough to bite him?"

"He went to help a farmer who had been bitten," explained Jacob.

They paused just by a well in the main square.

"It all started when the well dried up," said the boy in a hushed voice. "And strange noises started coming from it."

"Maybe Ravira is lurking down there," suggested Elenna.

Tom and Elenna peered down into the well.

"It's narrow enough to climb down," said Tom. "We can press our backs across one wall, our feet against the other."

A flicker of fear crossed Elenna's face.

"My father, Bo, was bitten," Jacob said suddenly. "He was the farmer your father went to help. He has a scar on his cheek. Please look out for him."

Tom assured him they would do what they could and then they lowered themselves down.

It was slow going. Tom was feeling tired when stones began falling onto them from above.

Elenna lost her balance and fell, smashing into Tom. He lost his grip and they both dropped like stones into the blackness. A moment later, they were sliding down a muddy slope. Shocked and winded, Tom tried to slow himself down as he caught sight of something terrifying straight ahead. It was a bubbling pool of fire. With desperate force, he managed to sink his sword into the mud and gradually came to a halt.

Elenna slammed into him. Trembling, they got to their feet and stared at the lake of lava in front of them.

"This way," said Tom, pointing along a path made from polished white rock.

"It must lead to Ravira."

Together, they walked through the swirling, stinking smoke.

Through the dim light, Tom made out a boat drifting towards them. It was manned by a figure in a dark cloak.

"Only those who have been bitten may cross to the queen's city," the figure snarled.

Tom thought fast. He pushed the tip of his sword into his leg.

"The Hounds have bitten us," said Tom, showing his wound.

The boatman pulled down his hood, revealing a pale scar down one side of his face.

"You're Jacob's father!" Elenna gasped.

The boatman shot out both hands, dragging Tom and Elenna into the boat. Trying not to panic, they felt themselves slowly moving

across the boiling lava.

"Duck!" shouted Tom, as arcs of flame shot through the air towards them. Howls and distant thunder echoed all around as the boatman eventually rounded a curve. A city of white stone appeared before them.

As the boat slid into the shallows, Tom and Elenna leapt out.

"Ravira's Hounds will tear you to pieces," warned the boatman, as he pushed back out onto the fiery lake.

"No turning back now," whispered Tom.

"This must be Ravira's lair," said Tom.

There was no sound as he led the way through the empty streets, towards a vast fortress up ahead. There was no sign of life anywhere either.

As they moved into the courtyard, it was darker. The air seemed thick with the smell of animals, like a stables or kennels. As they pressed on, weapons ready, a staircase rose ahead of them. At the very top was a huge throne. On it sat a statue.

"Ravira?" asked Tom.

"Welcome to the underworld," whispered a woman's voice.

As Ravira stood, Tom saw that she was at least seven feet tall. Her skin was tinged green and her eyes blazed yellow like flaming torches. Around the base of the steps, six Hounds of Avantia stood guard. They looked strong, with thick dark fur and teeth as sharp as daggers.

Tom held up his shield. Could they take on six of these creatures without killing them? They were, after all, citizens of Avantia who had been entranced by Ravira.

Ravira suddenly tipped her head back into a shaft of light. She was drawing power from the moonlight!

"We can't risk fighting the Hounds," Elenna said to Tom. "One bite, and we'll go the same way as your father."

"After them!" Ravira suddenly screamed, releasing the dogs from their leashes.

Tom grabbed Elenna's hand and they raced back out into the strange white city. The pack of snapping Hounds was right behind them.

Elenna pointed to a tall turret. "If we climb up, they won't be able to follow," she said, gasping.

They threw themselves against the wall, the Hounds on their heels. Feeling around for handholds, Tom and Elenna scrambled up the rough stone.

It wasn't long before Tom heard a terrible crumbling sound.

I FEEL THE POWER OF THE MOON OVER ME. I feel Ravira's spirit take me over completely. I am a man no more. I am Ravira's faithful servant, Taladon. Soon Ravira will reign over all!

PART TWO

WELCOME TO THE UNDERWORLD

WELCOME TO THE UNDERWORLD

He hit the ground hard. Dust filled his eyes and throat and rocks smashed into his limbs. He thought he could hear Elenna screaming. Then all was quiet.

"Elenna!" he called.

Tom tried to move his arms and legs. But he was trapped.

A shaft of light appeared through the fallen stones. Tom heard sounds coming from above.

Then Tom smelled the animal smell of the Hounds.

"No!" he suddenly heard Elenna whimper from nearby.

He reached for the hilt of his sword just as he felt a huge slab lifted away above his head.

Peering towards the light, Tom came face to face with one of Ravira's Hounds.

Drool dripped onto Tom's cheek as the Hound snapped its teeth into his arm. He cried out as the fangs sank through his skin.

"I've been bitten!" he called out, glancing down at the deep gashes on his arm.

Almost at once, a strange feeling spread down his arm, across his chest and through his body, right to the tips of his toes. The dog's eyes were filled with evil.

More Hounds appeared above Tom, pawing away the stones.

One of the drooling monsters leaned down and gripped the collar of Tom's tunic, dragging him from the rubble.

"Tom?" said Elenna.

Tom saw his friend held by another of the Hounds. Her clothes were torn and her face was covered in dust. Glancing down, he noticed the same teeth marks through her trousers.

"I feel different," she said.

A sense of dread came over Tom.

He wondered how long they had to save themselves, to save everyone, to defeat Ravira.

The Hounds dragged Tom and Elenna away from the tower and back towards the fortress... and their mistress.

A single column of moonlight shone down onto Ravira's throne. She pointed a bony finger at Tom and Elenna.

"Welcome back, my children!" she cackled. Tom saw that she held several leashes.

Another row of Hounds stood waiting by her throne.

"There are more than before," whispered Elenna.

"That's because more people are being bitten all the time," Tom replied.

"Meet your brothers and sisters," said Ravira.

Tom drew his sword and glared at the Evil Beast.

"While there's blood in my veins, I'll never be one of them," he shouted.

"The blood in your veins is already poisoned," replied Ravira, cruelly.

Suddenly, a bright shaft of moonlight fell directly onto Tom and Elenna. With a cry, Tom

shielded his eyes and dropped to his knees. They both writhed in pain as the light burned their skin.

"What is this?" said Tom.

"Just a taste of what is to come," said Ravira.

The Hounds snarled and strained on their leashes.

Tom felt desperate. There had to be a way to reach Ravira. If she was under some kind of enchantment, perhaps he could reason with her. "Why are you doing this?" he asked.

"Silence!" she hissed furiously.

As Ravira moved, just for a moment, out of the moonlight, Tom thought he caught sight of a younger woman – not like a Beast at all. As she moved back into the light, her skin wrinkled again before his eyes.

"You know nothing of my curse!" she whispered.

"The moonlight is the source of all her

power!" whispered Elenna.

Ravira gave a hissing laugh as a doorway beside her throne slid open. A Hound, bigger and more evil-looking than the others, slowly entered the chamber. The look in his eyes chilled Tom's blood.

"Tom," hissed Ravira. "Meet your father."

The Hound snarled and stared at Tom.

He was chained but was straining to get free.

"Father?" Tom said.

Tom lifted his shield and the Hound's teeth raked across it.

"Release him from his chains!" Tom shouted at Ravira.

As shafts of moonlight shone down through the roof, Tom felt more burning across his skin. He could see Elenna falling to her knees in pain too. As the feeling increased, anger rose up in Tom. Hatred boiled in his heart.

I'm changing, he realised. *And there's nothing I can do.*

"Do you feel it yet?" Ravira smiled. "The thirst for blood?"

As Ravira spoke, Tom noticed something terrible.

"Elenna! Your mouth!"

His friend turned to him. Her teeth were growing longer and sharper. Her face was changing too, in front of his eyes!

"It's time to join the pack!" Ravira laughed.

Pain stabbed across Tom's chest as he saw his father stalking towards him. There had to be some way to stop this. He had to block out the moonlight.

As his father, the Hound, pounced, his face was full of hatred. Reaching for his sword, Tom felt a sudden urge to hurt him.

"Remember, he's your father!" gasped Elenna, just in time.

Suddenly, Tom opened his eyes and saw the shape of a huge wing hovering high above.

"Ferno!" called Tom.

The great friendly Beast had come to their rescue. He must have sensed their fear. The bulk

Welcome to the Underworld

of the huge dragon kept out the moonlight almost completely.

"What's happening?" Ravira cried. "Hounds! Attack!"

They tried to fight off the Hounds but time was running out. Tom felt his hopes die.

"Your Quest is over!" cackled Ravira above the growling of her Hounds. She was standing in the last shaft of moonlight. "You won't defeat me!"

The Hounds whined in fear as the great Beast flapped his wings overhead and the chamber became dark. One Hound didn't seem as afraid as the others, and took a step towards Tom. *Taladon!*

"I don't want to fight you," said Tom. But he was ready when the animal jumped towards him.

Tom had no choice. He thrust his sword into his father's side. The creature fell to the ground.

"What have I done?" Tom said quietly.

"Call off your dragon, and I'll spare your lives!" spat Ravira.

"Never!" replied Tom.

Using his shield, Tom forged a path through the mass of Hounds. He had just reached Ravira's throne when he was thrown to the ground. He twisted round to see a Hound with its teeth gripping his trouser leg. It dragged him across the ground while he kicked it with the other foot. At last it let go.

"There are too many of them!" shouted Elenna. She was slashing at the Beasts to keep them at bay.

Welcome to the Underworld

"I think Ravira's power is linked to the Hounds as well as the moonlight," Tom replied. "The more Hounds she has, the stronger she is." He swung his sword once more.

"If I can help you past the Hounds," said Tom to Elenna, "you cut through the leashes."

He roared as the tip of his sword scraped across the stone floor, sending up a shower of sparks. The Hounds retreated in fear.

"Now!" Tom shouted.

Elenna took a few steps, then she bounded over the Hounds and up the steps towards Ravira.

"Stop her!" yelled the Beast, as Elenna

brought Taladon's sword down onto the chains.

The leashes burst apart. The Hounds stopped snarling. Their angry red eyes faded to soft grey.

"They're no longer under her control," Elenna said.

Ravira roared in fury.

"I will come back for you," Tom called to his father, as they quickly backed out of the chamber.

The Beast lashed at them with the spiked leashes. Tom and Elenna managed to catch the

chains around their swords, dragging Ravira with them. Soon they were outside again and nearing the lava lake.

"I'll tear you to pieces!" Ravira shouted. The Beast had turned now, and was trying to pull Tom and Elenna towards her. They pulled back hard, and then let the chains go slack.

With a panicked cry, Ravira lost her balance and fell, screaming, into the boiling lake.

Tom turned back at once. He had to save his father.

When they arrived at the fortress, the Hounds blocked their path. Tom took a risk.

"You're not evil, are you?" he whispered.

The creatures dropped to the ground, seeming to shrink. Their limbs changed shape and their faces turned human again. Soon the chamber was filled with confused people. One of them was Taladon.

"How can we get out?" asked Elenna. No one wanted to cross the lava lake. Who knew what power Ravira still held?

Welcome to the Underworld

"Follow us," said a voice. It was Bo, leading the saved people. "There is another way."

The weary group followed Bo along a low, dark passage until at last they saw light ahead. Bo pushed open a trap door and they

were back in the village.

Riding towards them on Storm was Jacob.

"Your horse wouldn't stop whinnying!" he said. "He seemed to know you'd be here!"

"My son!" said Bo, as they were happily reunited at last.

"Avantia's underworld is the darkest place," said a voice. Aduro was walking towards them. "But I know that with heroes such as you fighting for it, Avantia is well protected."

"Farewell, friends," called Tom to Bo, Jacob and the villagers. "Now we must go home."

Dear Quester,

Well done for completing these Quests with me and Elenna. We couldn't have kept Avantia safe without your help.

Something tells me this will not be our last adventure together, though. While there's blood in my veins, and Elenna and I have you on our side, we will keep the kingdom safe from Evil.

Tom

Beast Quest

Join Tom and Elenna on their first Beast Quests!

TOP TRUMPS COLLECTOR CARDS INSIDE! FREE

978 1 84616 483 5

978 1 84616 482 8

978 1 84616 484 2

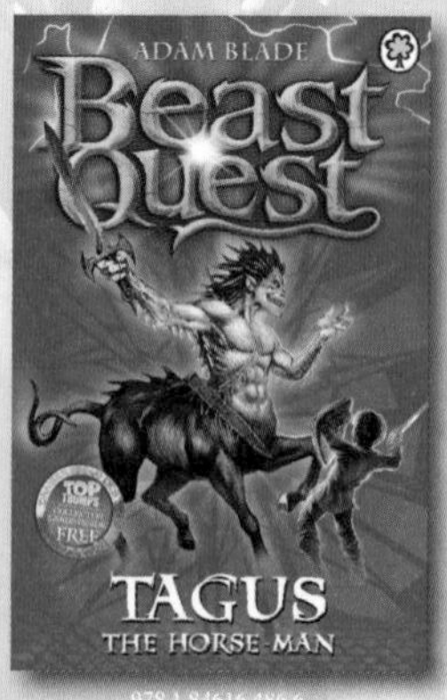

978 1 84616 486 6

978 1 84616 485 9

978 1 84616 487 3

All the facts you need to become
Master of the Beasts!

ISBN: 978 1 40833 839 1